Piglet was excited. It was Christmas Eve and that meant Santa Claus would soon be here!

Piglet was busy decorating his home for Santa's arrival when suddenly he became worried.

Christopher Robin had told Piglet that every year
Santa and his reindeer flew around the world with
presents for everyone who had been good.

But Piglet was concerned. After all, the world was
such a big place, and he was just a little piglet.

"Oh, dear," he cried. "What if Santa forgets me?"

Piglet decided he needed help. So he put on his hat and scarf, snuffed out the candles, and hurried to see Winnie the Pooh.

"I must talk to you, Pooh," Piglet said
as soon as he arrived at the bear's house.
"It's very important."

Pooh invited his little friend in.

"Pooh," Piglet started shyly, "what if Santa forgets to visit my house? What if he's too busy to bring me a present?"

"Santa has never forgotten you before, Piglet," Pooh said.

"But he might!" Piglet cried. "I'm so little."

"Oh, but Piglet, you're too special to forget," Pooh said.

"Promise?" Piglet asked.

"Promise," answered Pooh.

This made Piglet very happy. His best
friend had made him a promise. Now things
couldn't go wrong. He thanked Pooh and
went home to finish his decorations.

Pooh was glad he had helped his friend. But soon he, too, became worried. What if Santa did forget? After all, Pooh forgot things all the time.

What was a Pooh
to do? He couldn't
disappoint his best
friend—*a promise
is a promise!*

"I know!" Pooh said
at last. "I shall ask my
friends what to do."

So Pooh hurried to Rabbit's house.

"Hello, Rabbit, and Merry Christmas!"
Pooh called out.

"Hello, Pooh," answered Rabbit.
"And the same to you!"

Pooh told Rabbit about his promise to Piglet.

"What should I do?"
Pooh asked.

"Well, a promise *is* a promise," Rabbit answered.
"But I don't know how to help you keep it."

Then Pooh went to see Eeyore.

"Hello, Eeyore," said Pooh. "Merry Christmas!"

"Well, the snow hasn't knocked over my house yet," Eeyore said with a sigh. "So I suppose it could be worse."

Pooh told him what he had promised Piglet, but Eeyore couldn't help him, either.

"If you break a promise, it'll be a gloomy Christmas," Eeyore sighed.

After hearing Eeyore's glum words,
Pooh needed cheering up. So he went to
the happy home of Kanga and Roo.

"Let's help, Mama!" Roo cried after
hearing Pooh's story.

"I would love to," said Kanga. "But I
simply don't know how we can be sure
Santa won't forget Piglet."

Poor Pooh! His little brain hurt from
thinking. His empty tummy rumbled.
And then he was bounced to the ground!

"Hello to you, Pooh!" cried Tigger. "Why so glum, chum?"

Pooh told Tigger his problem.

"I'll just have to wait and see whether Santa gives Piglet a present," Pooh said.

"Tiggers never wait!" Tigger replied. "Ya gotta have a plan, and lucky for you, making plans is what tiggers do best!"

Pooh and Tigger came up with a plan.
But they needed help. So they went to
visit Rabbit.

"Hello again, Rabbit," said Pooh.

"Listen up, Long Ears," said Tigger.
"Me and the bear got us a t-riffic plan to
help Piglet."

"You do?" asked Rabbit.

"We do?" asked Pooh.

"Sure do," Tigger answered. "But we need help."

"From me?" replied Rabbit suspiciously.

"It's Christmas!" said Tigger. "You wouldn't turn down a pal at Christmastime. Would you?"

"Uh … well, no … but …"

"You did say a promise is a promise," Pooh reminded him.

Rabbit didn't have much choice. He agreed to help.

Then Pooh and Tigger went to tell
Eeyore their plan.

"Would you help us, Eeyore?"
Pooh asked.

"You wouldn't want me," Eeyore
answered.

"Oh, but I think we would," Pooh said.

"I would probably ruin everything,"
Eeyore moaned.

"No, you wouldn't, pal!" Tigger said.

"I wouldn't?" Eeyore asked.

Then something amazing happened. Eeyore brightened up. He nearly even smiled.

"Okay," Eeyore said. "I'll do it."

Finally Pooh and Tigger visited Kanga
and Roo.

"We have a plan to help Piglet," Pooh
said to Kanga. "Will you help us?"

"Of course we will,"
Kanga said, smiling.

"Oh, boy!" Roo cried. "I could draw a picture of Piglet. See? I'm good at art!"

"What do you want us to do?" Kanga asked.

"Just follow me!" Tigger cried. "Hoo! Hoo!"

Soon, all the friends had gathered at Pooh's house. Each of them had brought some sticks. Tigger held an old antler-shaped coatrack.

"Why did you ask us to bring these silly sticks?" asked Rabbit.

"You'll see," Tigger answered. "Hey, Pooh, go get the surprise."

"Oh, bother!" Pooh said. "I know it's here ... somewhere."

Pooh soon found what he was looking for.

"Here it is!" Pooh cried. "Santa's sleigh!"

"That's not Santa's sleigh," Kanga said.

"It doesn't even look like Santa's sleigh!" Rabbit complained.

"It will when I'm finished with it!" Tigger cried.

And so the friends started to work on the
old sled. Tigger brought out an old box.

Then they cut out pieces of the box and placed them on the sides of the sled.

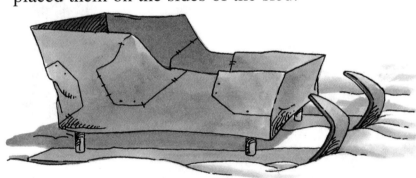

Finally they painted it.

Before they knew it, Santa's
sleigh was finished.

"We did it," Roo said.

"We double did it!" cried Tigger.

"I have to admit, it looks
good," Rabbit added.

"Now all we need is Santa
Claus himself!" Roo cried.

"Hoo hoo! That's your cue,
Pooh," Tigger said. "Get
the costume."

MR. SANDERS

RNIG
ALSO

Pooh pulled out a big old bag. He put on
a red hat and a white beard. He looked just
like … well, almost like Santa Claus!

"I shall be
Santa, and you
will all be my
reindeer!"

"What?" Rabbit cried.
"I'm not a reindeer!"
"The sticks will help you look
like one," Tigger explained.
So the friends tied the sticks to their
heads to look like antlers.

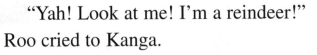

"Yah! Look at me! I'm a reindeer!"
Roo cried to Kanga.

"I'm in front!" Tigger cried. "Pulling
sleighs is what tiggers do best!"

"Ready, reindeer?" Pooh asked.

"Don't call me a reindeer!" Rabbit cried.

At last the friends were on their way.
But it was getting dark, and it was hard
to see the path to Piglet's house.

Still, Pooh was eager to keep his
promise to Piglet.

"We're almost there," Pooh cried.
"Faster, reindeer!"

"I said, don't call me a reindeer!"
Rabbit cried.

"You want fast? I'll give you fast, Santa
Pooh!" Tigger cried.

Suddenly Tigger shot ahead like a rocket!

Tigger ran so fast that Pooh and the presents fell off the sleigh! Oh, bother!

"Are you all right, Pooh?" Kanga asked.

"I think I am," Pooh answered. "At least some of me is."

"I told you I wasn't a reindeer!" Rabbit scolded.

The friends were so busy they did not
notice a strange object flying across the
sky. Or the sound of jingling bells.

Just then, Piglet's front door opened
a crack.

"W-who's there?" asked a scared little voice.

"Oh, what a pleasant surprise!" squealed Piglet
when he saw his friends at his doorstep. Then
he invited them all inside for Christmas treats.

"I'm sorry, Piglet," Pooh said sadly. "I didn't
keep my promise. Santa forgot you."

"Oh, but Pooh, you did keep your promise!"
Piglet cried. "Look, Santa came while I was asleep!"

It was true. Piglet's tree was surrounded
by presents.

"But you all went to so much trouble just
for me!" Piglet said. "That's the best present
of all. Merry Christmas, everyone!"

Rabbits Howse

Piglet

Nise For Snowballs

Snow pit where Roo playe

Owl

Pooh Bears Howse

Slushy Place

100 Aker Wood